There Was a Crooked Man

Distributed by The Child's World®
1980 Lookout Drive • Mankato, MN 56003-1705
800-599-READ • www.childsworld.com

Acknowledgments
The Child's World®: Mary Berendes, Publishing Director
The Design Lab: Kathleen Petelinsek, Design

Library of Congress Cataloging-in-Publication Data
Rooney, Ronnie.
There was a crooked man / illustrated by Ronnie Rooney.
    p. cm.
ISBN 978-1-60954-283-2 (library bound: alk. paper)
1. Nursery rhymes. 2. Children's poetry. [1. Nursery rhymes.] I. Title.
PZ8.3.R6652Th 2011
398.8—dc22
[E]   2010032418

Printed in the United States of America in Mankato, Minnesota.
December 2010
PA02073

ILLUSTRATED BY RONNIE ROONEY

There was a crooked
man, who walked a
crooked mile.

He found a crooked
sixpence upon a
crooked stile.

He bought a
crooked cat,

which caught a
crooked mouse.

And they all lived together in a little crooked house.

ABOUT MOTHER GOOSE

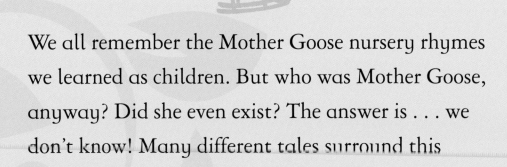

We all remember the Mother Goose nursery rhymes we learned as children. But who was Mother Goose, anyway? Did she even exist? The answer is . . . we don't know! Many different tales surround this famous name.

Some people think she might be based on Goose-footed Bertha, a kindly old woman in French legend who told stories to children. The inspiration for this legend might have been Queen Bertha of France, who died in 783 and whose son Charlemagne ruled much of Europe. Queen Bertha was called Big-footed Bertha or Queen Goosefoot because one foot was larger than the other.

The name "Mother Goose" first appeared in Charles Perrault's *Les Contes de ma Mère l'Oye* ("Tales of My Mother Goose"), published in France in 1697. This was a collection of fairy tales including "Cinderella" and "Sleeping Beauty"—but these were stories, not poems. The first published Mother Goose nursery rhymes appeared in England in 1781, as *Mother Goose's Melody; or Sonnets for the Cradle*. But some of the verses themselves are hundreds of years old, passed along by word of mouth.

Although we don't really know the origins of Mother Goose or her nursery rhymes, we *do* know that these timeless verses are beloved by children everywhere!

ABOUT THE ILLUSTRATOR

Ronnie Rooney was born and raised in Massachusetts. She attended the University of Massachusetts at Amherst for her undergraduate study and Savannah College of Art and Design for her MFA in illustration. In the last three years, she moved to Georgia, got married, got a dog, and had a baby girl—in that order!

Rooney has illustrated numerous books for children. She enjoys painting and drawing so much, that she would paint and draw all day even if she didn't get paid for it. She hopes to pass this love of art on to her little girl.